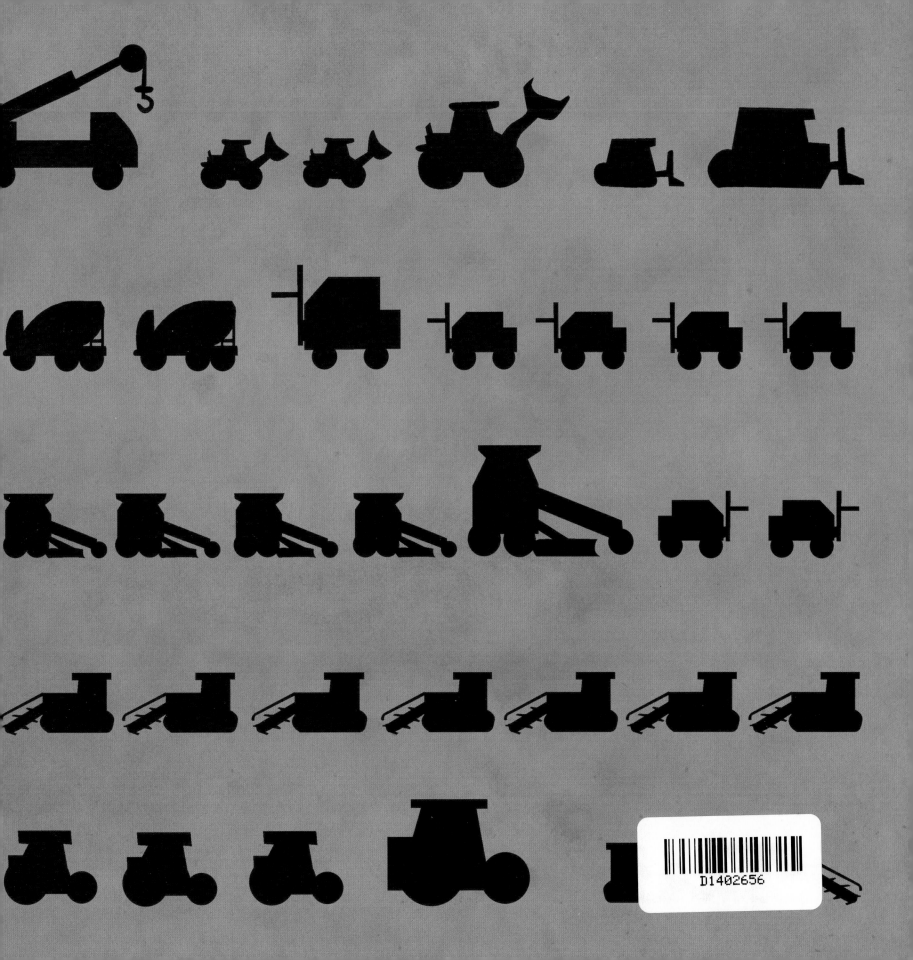

To Charlotte and William, Love Papa
—B. W.

For my brother, Ross
—C. L.

STERLING CHILDREN'S BOOKS
New York

An Imprint of Sterling Publishing Co., Inc.
1166 Avenue of the Americas
New York, NY 10036

ISBN 978-1-4549-2229-2

Distributed in Canada by Sterling Publishing Co., Inc.
c/o Canadian Manda Group, 664 Annette Street
Toronto, Ontario M6S 2C8, Canada
Distributed in the United Kingdom by GMC Distribution Services
Castle Place, 166 High Street, Lewes, East Sussex BN7 1XU, England
Distributed in Australia by NewSouth Books
45 Beach Street, Coogee NSW 2034, Australia

For information about custom editions, special sales,
and premium and corporate purchases, please contact
Sterling Special Sales at 800-805-5489 or
specialsales@sterlingpublishing.com.

Manufactured in China

Lot #:
2 4 6 8 10 9 7 5 3 1
02/18

sterlingpublishing.com

Cover and interior design by Irene Vandervoort

Over at the Construction Site

Over at the Construction Site

By Bill Wise

illustrated by Claire Lordon

STERLING CHILDREN'S BOOKS
New York

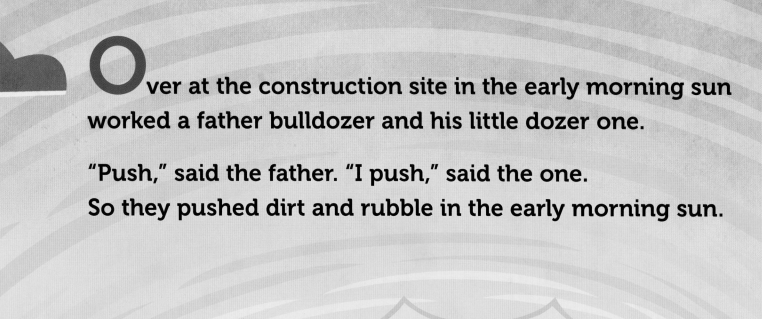

Over at the construction site in the early morning sun worked a father bulldozer and his little dozer one.

"Push," said the father. "I push," said the one.
So they pushed dirt and rubble in the early morning sun.

Over at the construction site where the sky gleams blue
worked a mother front loader and her little loaders two.

"Load," said the mother.
"We load," said the two.
So they loaded sand and rocks
where the sky gleams blue.

Over at the construction site
by an old pine tree
worked a father boom truck
and his little boomers three.

"Reach," said the father.
"We reach," said the three.
So they reached way up high
to the old pine tree.

Over at the construction site where there's noise you can't ignore
worked a mother dump truck and her little dumpers four.

"Tip," said the mother.
"We tip," said the four.
So they tipped and they dumped
where there's noise you can't ignore.

Over at the construction site where the big trucks drive
worked a father cement mixer and his little mixers five.

"Mix," said the father.
"We mix," said the five.
So they mixed and they poured
where the big trucks drive.

Over at the construction site near a hundred tons of bricks
worked a mother forklift and her little lifters six.

"Lift," said the mother.
"We lift," said the six.
So they lifted and they moved
the hundred tons of bricks.

Over at the construction site where the motors are revvin' worked a father grader truck and his little graders seven.

"Scrape," said the father. "We scrape," said the seven.
So they scraped and they leveled where the motors are revvin'.

Over at the construction site where the crew stays late
worked a mother digger truck and her little diggers eight.

"Dig," said the mother. "We dig," said the eight.
So they dug and they scooped where the crew stays late.

Over at the construction site near the "keep out" sign
worked a father trencher truck and his little trenchers nine.

"Cut," said the father. "We cut," said the nine.
So they cut a long trench near the "keep out" sign.

Over at the construction site where it's hot now and then
worked a mother roller truck and her little rollers ten.

"Roll," said the mother. "We roll," said the ten.
So they rolled sand and tar where it's hot now and then.

Over at the construction site, let's look and see what's there.
It's a brand new school built with lots of pride and care!

"Celebrate," said the adult trucks. "The job was well done."
So they all celebrated underneath the setting sun.

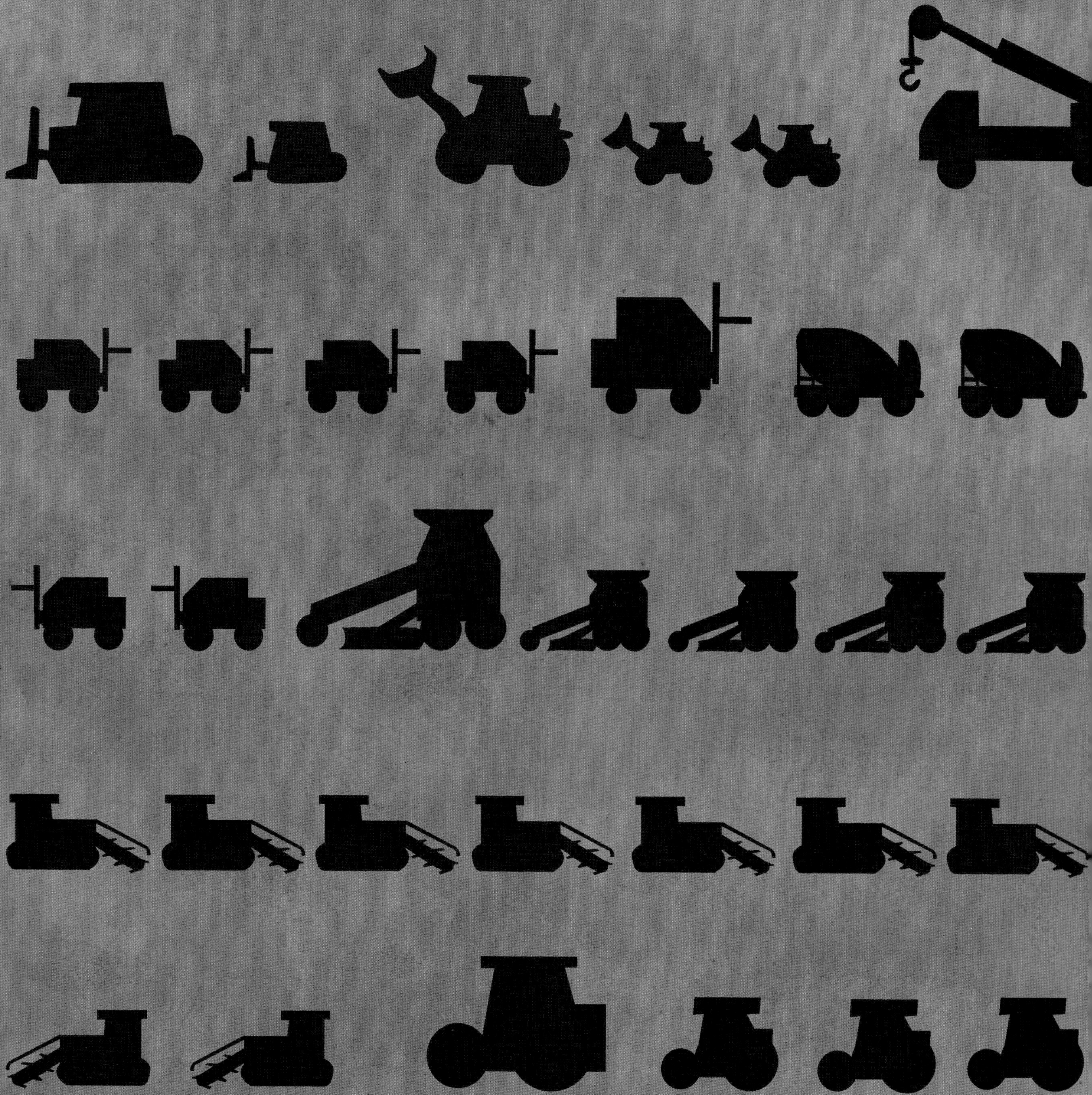